How to Draw Deltora Monsters

Marc McBride
Emily Rodda

Scholastic Inc.

New York   Toronto   London   Auckland   Sydney
Mexico City   New Delhi   Hong Kong   Buenos Aires

Foreword

Marc McBride's wonderful cover paintings for the Deltora Quest series, and his illustrations in *The Deltora Book of Monsters*, have inspired thousands of children all over the world. I know from the letters I receive that many readers like to draw the monsters they meet in the books.

Now Marc has gone one step further. He has produced this book that shows exactly how he creates his masterpieces—so you can re-create them, too!

Emily Rodda

Emily Rodda

We draw to express our ideas and to show our ideas to other people. A drawing can also be a key to unlock our imagination and take us on a journey. There are no rules when it comes to drawing—everyone has a different style and method. The only real way to become better at drawing is to practice. If you go through each step in this book with me, you will end up with your very own set of Deltora monsters. Following these steps will also make it easier for you to create your own.

When you color each monster, think about what mood you want to express. Different colors can help achieve different effects—some colors make us feel happy, others sad. Also, some are hot, and some are cold. There is no right or wrong about which colors you use. But there are two basic rules—colors get lighter as they get further away; and you should start with lighter colors before gradually adding the darker ones. Learn from your mistakes. For example, when I spilled green paint over a picture and dabbed it off with a cloth, I discovered a great new way to create trees! Like any journey, painting can be more fun when you don't know exactly where you are going. I never know what a painting will look like until it is finished.

Come and have some fun drawing Deltora monsters with me.

Marc McBride

Contents

Gorl   4–7

Soldeen   8–11

Vraal   12–15

Ak-Baba   16–19

Muddlet   20–23

Sand Beast   24–27

Dragon   28–31

Gellick   32–35

The Glus   36–39

Reeah   40–43

Color Drawing   44–47

Gorl

Gorl is a fearsome knight, clad in the golden battle armor of the Jalis tribe.
He guards the dark center of Mid Wood in the Forests of Silence,
slaying anyone who tries to enter his domain.

Instructions

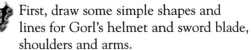

First, draw some simple shapes and lines for Gorl's helmet and sword blade, shoulders and arms.

Draw in the upper torso (chest) area.

Now sketch in the gauntlets, shoulder armor, and outline for the chain-mail tunic.

Next, draw the legs and boots, sword handle, shoulder detail, and helmet horns.

Instructions

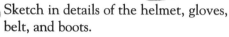

Sketch in details of the helmet, gloves, belt, and boots.

Add more detail to Gorl's armor and provide him with a place to stand.

Add shading and fine detail—for example, entwined Celtic vine shapes, the skull on the belt, and the goat skulls on the kneecaps. Sketch in a background.

Color your drawing using yellows and browns, with white highlights to give a metallic look to the armor.

Variations

Soldeen

Soldeen lurks in the murky depths of the Lake of Tears. Created by the sorceress Thaegan, he can breathe both air and water and is able to speak.

Instructions

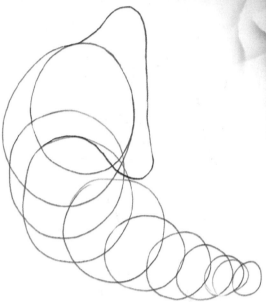

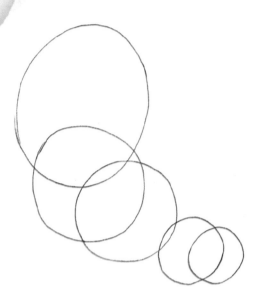

 Draw a series of five overlapping circles, as shown.

 Draw in more circles, and add the outline of the gaping mouth.

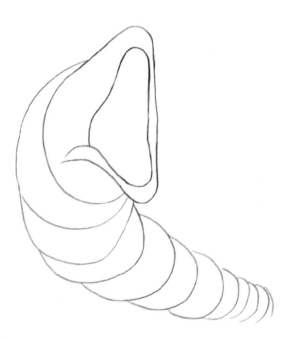

 Erase the inside parts of the circles, so that a worm-like body begins to emerge. Add the inside line of the mouth.

 Add the eye, teeth, inner mouth detail, and some semicircular lines to the side of the head. Draw more interlocking circles as shown—these will become the back part of the body.

9

Instructions

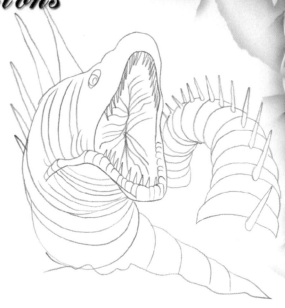

Erase the inside parts of the interlocking circles that you drew in Step 4. Add more curved lines to that part of the body. Sketch in the waterline.

Add the spines to Soldeen's head and back. Add more detail to the mouth and jawline.

Draw membranes between the spines and more details to the head, adding spiky whiskers to the cheek. Draw in the surface of the lake.

Add texture and shading, especially to the head and mouth. Color Soldeen green, and add light yellow highlights to give a shimmering, eel-like luster to the skin.

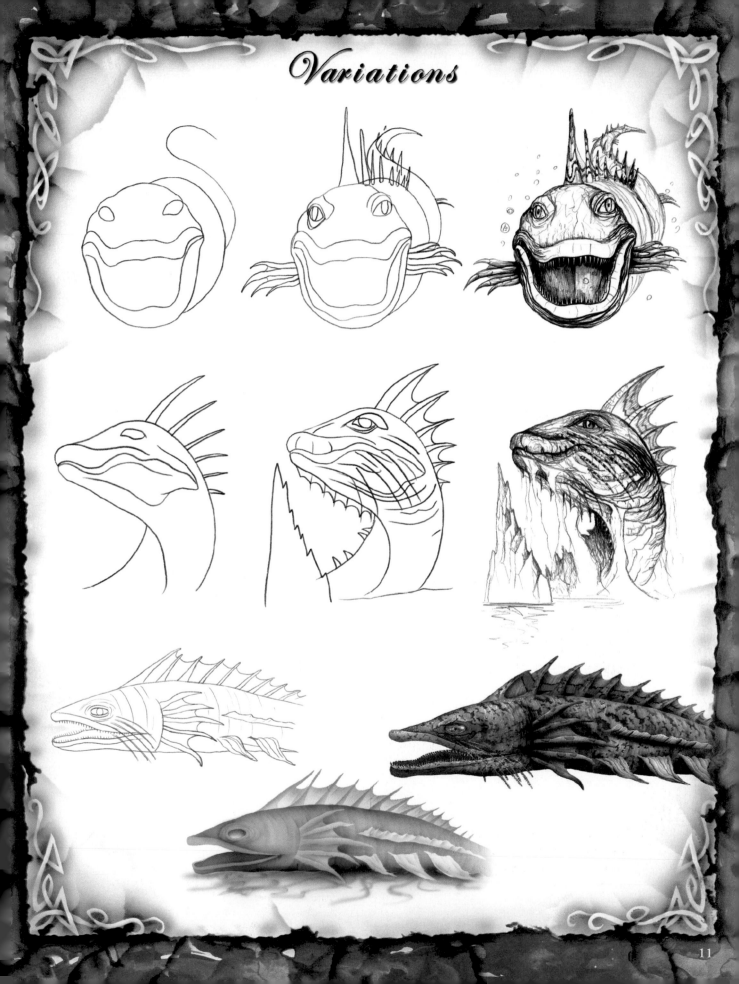

Vraal

Vraal are vicious fighting beasts bred in the Shadowlands for the purpose of combat.
They live only to fight and destroy, and are highly intelligent in the ways of battle.

Instructions

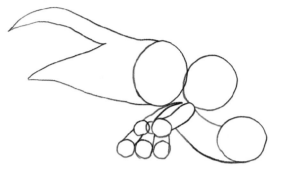

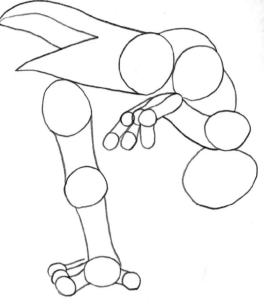

Begin with small circles and simple lines to make an outline of the Vraal's head and left hand.

Draw more circles and join them up with lines for the right arm and hand, as well as for the left arm and knee.

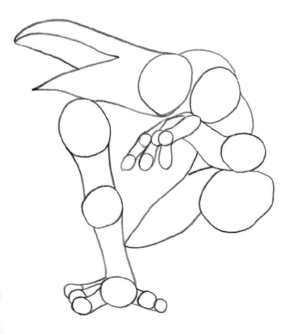

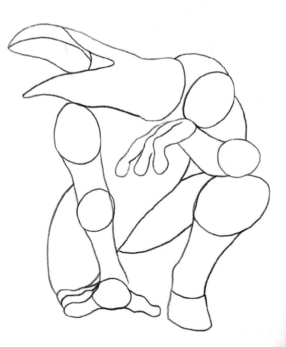

Finish the torso and left thigh.

Erase the small pencil circles from the hands. Add detail to the mouth and sketch in the legs.

Instructions

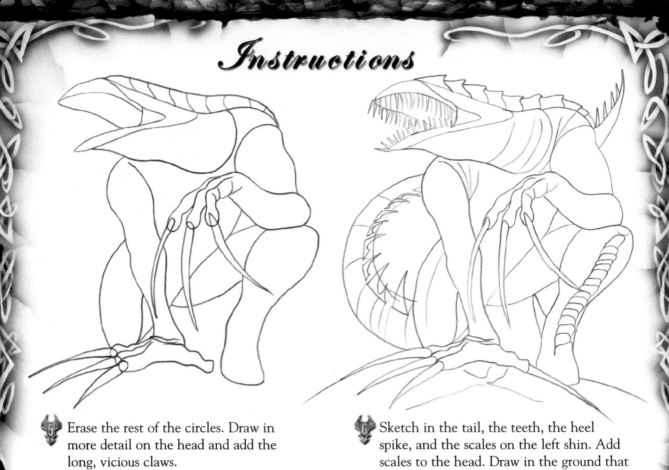

5 Erase the rest of the circles. Draw in more detail on the head and add the long, vicious claws.

6 Sketch in the tail, the teeth, the heel spike, and the scales on the left shin. Add scales to the head. Draw in the ground that the Vraal is standing on.

7 Add lots of criss-cross lines to bring out the Vraal's scaly, crocodile-like skin. Give your drawing texture by adding shading. Add background.

8 Add color, using greens, browns, and other earth colors that would provide the Vraal with camouflage in the Shadowlands.

Variations

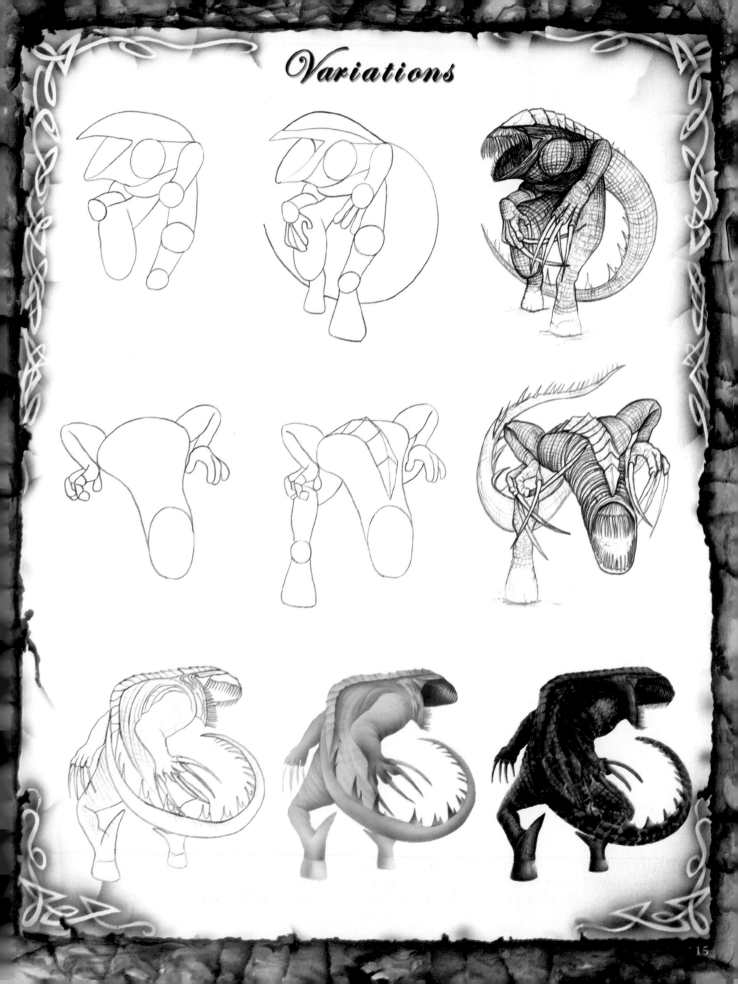

Ak-Baba

The seven Ak-Baba, ferocious servants of the Shadow Lord, were bred from wild
Ak-Baba, huge vulture-like birds said to live a thousand years. They feed on
both the living and the dead.

Instructions

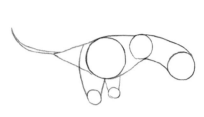

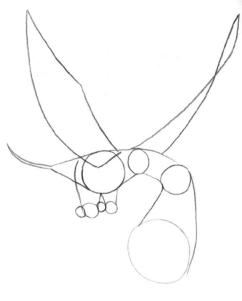

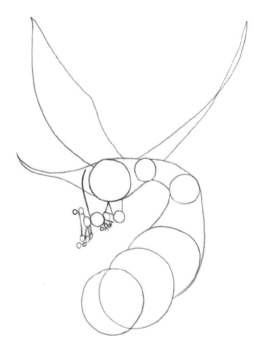

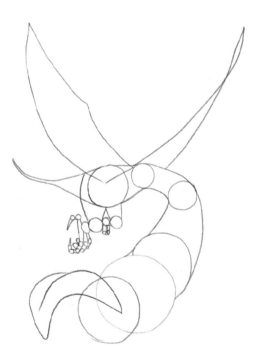

Start off by drawing five circles, some connecting lines, and a little tail.

Add other circles and lines, as shown, and sketch in two wings.

Insert another two interlocking circles on the front of the body. Erase the overlapped lines. Draw in the Ak-Baba's talons.

Add a shape for the mighty beak and continue working on the talons.

Instructions

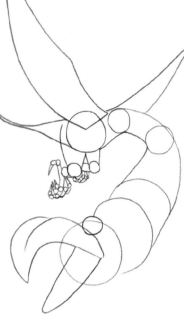

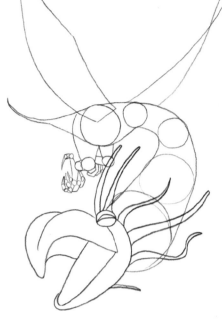

Sketch in the bottom jaw. Add a small circle for the eye.

Begin the trailing frill of spines on the neck. Develop the ferocious eye.

Sketch in the wing feathers and the vulture-like hair at the base of the neck. Add spikes along the back and more frilly spines to the neck. Draw in detail for the mouth. Add more lines to the body.

Add teeth and more intricate details to the wing feathers. Complete your Ak-Baba with color and shading.

Muddlet

Muddlets are good-natured but unreliable beasts. They eat only grass, moss, apples, and certain leaves. They can travel at high speeds, but are very stubborn and can lead their riders into grave danger.

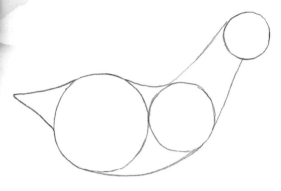

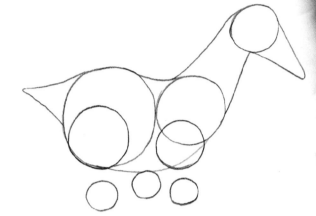

 Draw two circles, one bigger than the other. Add a smaller one above them. Join the circles with connecting lines and add a triangle for the stumpy tail.

 Add more circles as indicated. Draw another triangle for the nose.

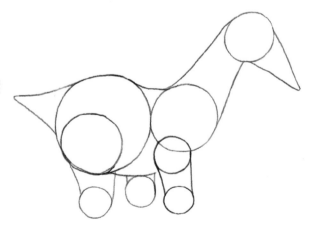

 Join each lower circle to the circle above it, for the top of the three legs.

 Extend the legs using three more small circles and connecting lines.

Instructions

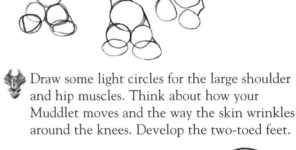

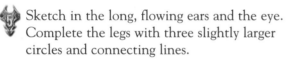

Sketch in the long, flowing ears and the eye. Complete the legs with three slightly larger circles and connecting lines.

Draw some light circles for the large shoulder and hip muscles. Think about how your Muddlet moves and the way the skin wrinkles around the knees. Develop the two-toed feet.

Give more definition to the overall body shape. Work on the eye, ears, and feet. Add richly patterned skin, like a zebra, a tiger, or even a leaf pattern—your choice!

Color in your Muddlet, and remember: Each Muddlet is different. Be creative.

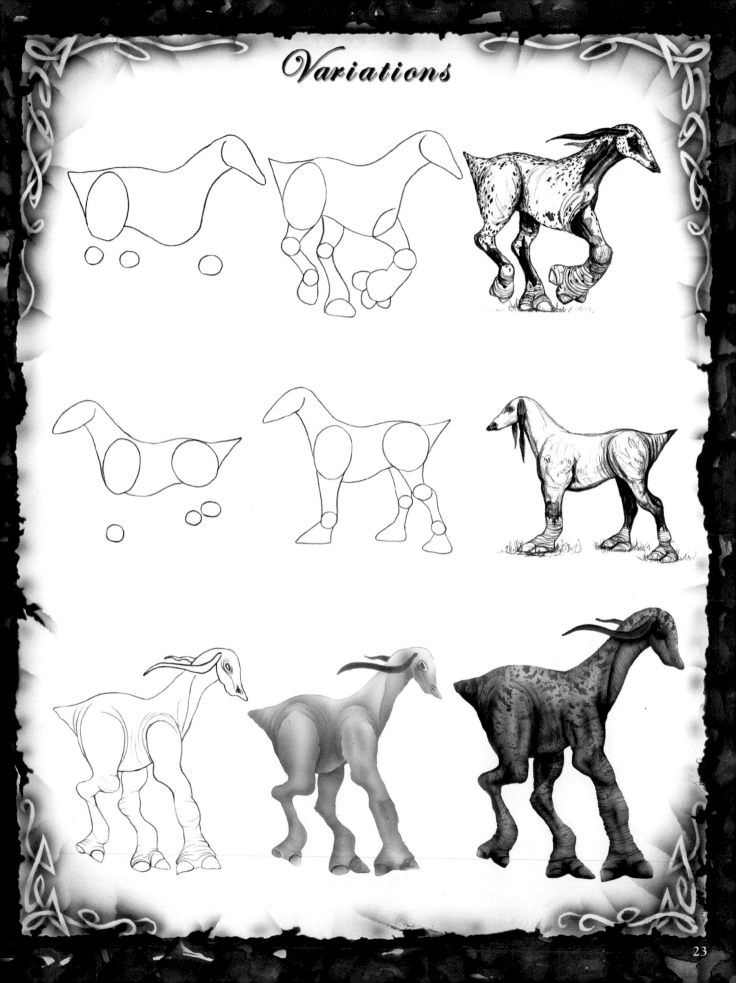

Sand Beast

Sand Beasts are huge and ferocious hunters who prowl the Shifting Sands in search of prey.
They have several leathery, grape-like stomachs that fall from their bodies when full.
The stomachs are then pierced and eggs laid inside them.

Instructions

Start off with a rough sketch of the eyes, head, and body.

Add small circles to the shoulder area and sketch in the crescent-moon-shaped hips.

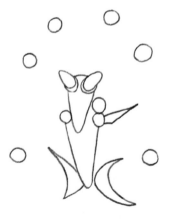

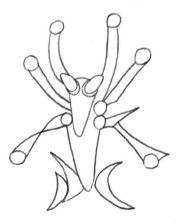

Add six small circles spaced around the body like juggling balls. These will become the arms and legs.

Join these six circles to the body and draw a smaller crescent-moon shape on the right hip.

Instructions

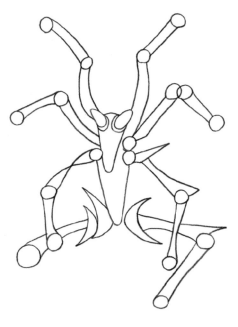

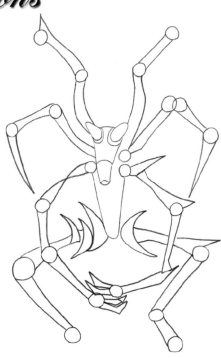

Add more circles and lines for the arms and legs.

Keep working on the arms and legs. Add spikes and claws, and begin working on the face.

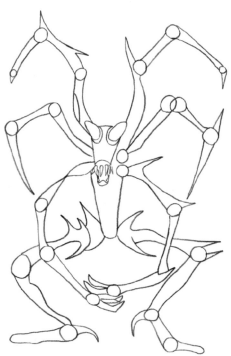

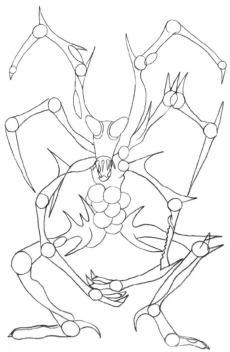

Complete the feet. Finish off the upper arms. Make sure you include all the spiky joints. Finish off the face.

Add more spikes, as shown. Draw in the creature's bunch of leathery, grape-like stomachs. (It can have between four and sixteen!)

Instructions

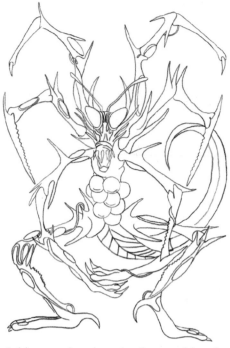

9 Draw jagged edges on the pincers of the middle arms and lower legs. Sketch in the long curved tail.

10 Add more detail to the face and head, as well as to the tail, knees, and feet. Erase the circles at the various joints.

Finish off the face, head, and tail. Add shading and any details you've missed.

Use your imagination to color your Sand Beast various shades of brown. You can look to nature for inspiration: butterflies, beetles, or my favorite—sea creatures.

Dragon

The dragons of Deltora are divided into seven tribes—topaz, ruby, opal, lapis-lazuli, emerald, amethyst, and diamond. A dragon's prime color matches the gem of its territory, but its underside changes color with the sky to camouflage it during flight.

Instructions

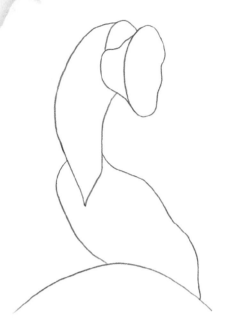

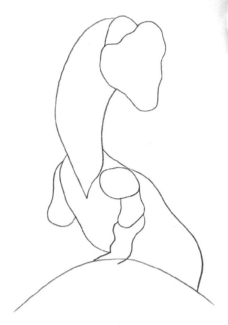

1 Outline the dragon's body, neck, and head. Draw a curved line to represent the ground.

2 Draw a circle for the right shoulder. Then start the front legs. Add the top part of the left arm.

3 Add some detail to the mouth and head. Sketch in the rest of the arms. Draw in the claws, using circles for the knuckles.

4 Add a line to the neck. Work on the teeth and the eye, and the scaly bone over the eye. Add talons to the claws.

Instructions

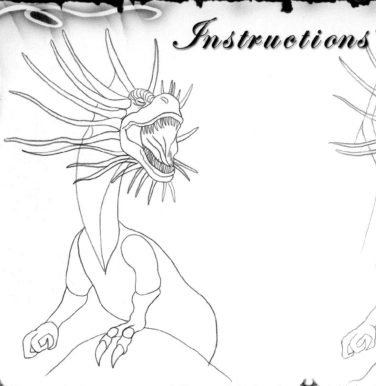

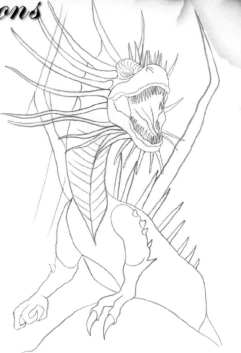

5 Draw in the long spines in a frill around the head.

6 Add detail to the neck segments. Add spikes to the upper arms and back, and begin the mighty wings. (I couldn't fit all of my dragon's wings on the page!)

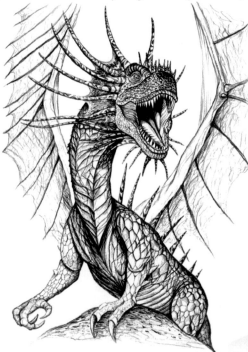

7 Add membranes to the wings and work on the dragon's scaly skin. Add shading. Look at lizards and other animals with scales to get ideas for the skin texture.

8 Sketch in the rocky ground and add a background. Don't forget that dragons can be many different colors. Use your imagination to make up your very own dragon species.

Gellick

The giant toad Gellick lives in Dread Mountain. Poisonous slime oozes from its skin.
It is a vile beast, greedy, cruel, and swollen with conceit.

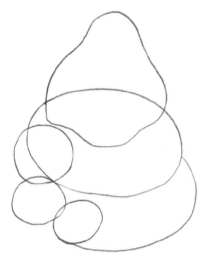

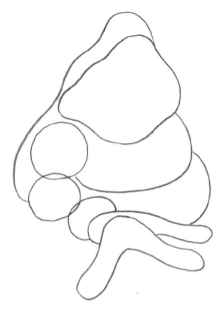

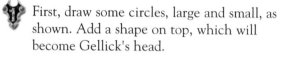

First, draw some circles, large and small, as shown. Add a shape on top, which will become Gellick's head.

Add a line to the head shape for the almost-closed mouth. Outline the three-toed foot.

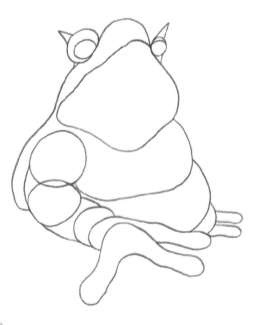

Sketch in the protruding eyes and the visible part of the left foot. Join the circles and outline the shape of the arm. Add triangular shapes to the top of the eyes.

Give the swollen stomach its wrinkles by adding cross-lines. Add claws to the toes. Draw in the sticky tongue and put some small spikes on Gellick's back. Build up the back part of the body.

Instructions

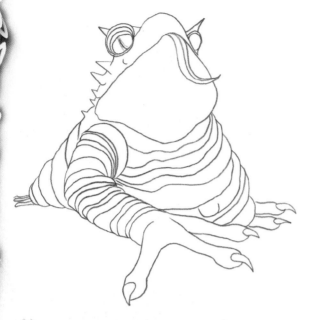

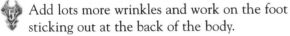

5 Add lots more wrinkles and work on the foot sticking out at the back of the body.

6 Sketch in the treasure lying on the ground. Add the wart-like bulges to Gellick's body and draw in the ridges under his chin.

7 Add more detail to the body and head. Shade the line of the mouth and work on the eyes.

8 Add background. Color Gellick's body in browns and yellows, with red and green markings on his arms.

Variations

The Glus

The Glus is a gigantic, slug-like beast. Its lair is the Maze of the Beast, beneath Deltora's western sea. Sickly pale and constantly on the hunt for food, it entraps prey by shooting sticky white threads from its mouth.

Instructions

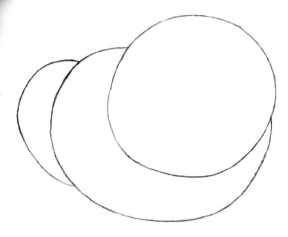

Begin the body by drawing three circles, one behind the other. Erase the inside lines.

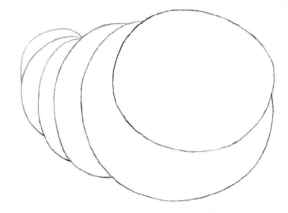

Add more circles for the long, slithery, slug-like body.

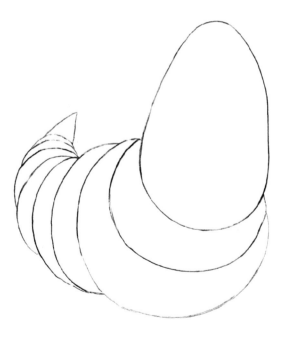

Draw a large egg shape for the head and draw a triangle shape at the back for the tail.

Add more rings and wrinkles to the body. Outline the gaping mouth.

Instructions

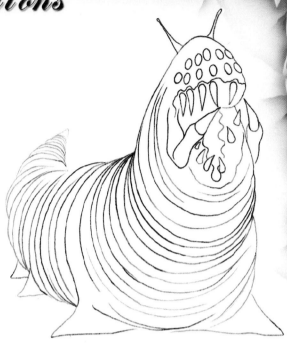

Draw in the feet, the teeth, and the fangs at the side of the mouth.

Develop the mouth. Add detail to the head, including the eye-stalks. Add more wrinkles.

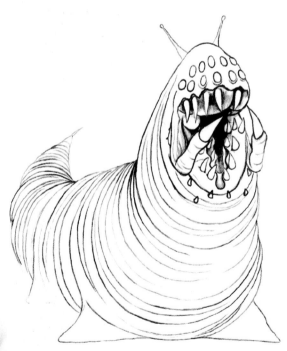

Keep working on the horrible mouth. Use shading to give it depth.

Color your Glus—a very pale blue for the body and blood-red for its huge mouth. You can emphasize the paleness of the body by adding a dark background—perhaps a gloomy cavern featuring stalagmites and stalactites.

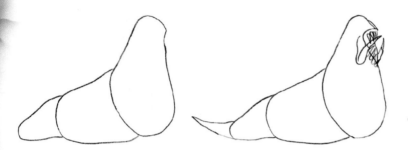

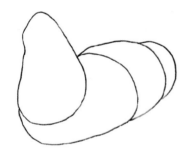

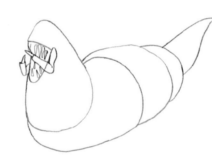

Reeah

Reeah is a giant snake. Its body is as thick as an ancient tree trunk and vast enough to fill a great hall. Its vanity and wickedness know no bounds.

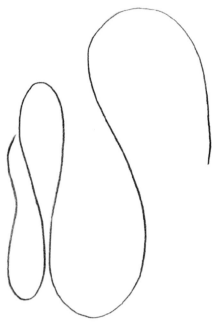

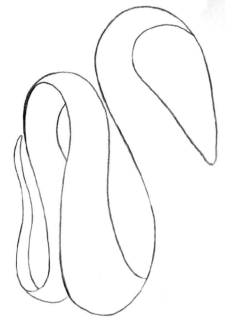

Make sure your pencil fits comfortably in your hand—not too tight, not too loose. Draw this sinuous shape with one smooth movement.

Make a rounded triangular shape for Reeah's head. Then outline the tail and body.

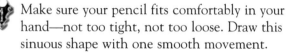

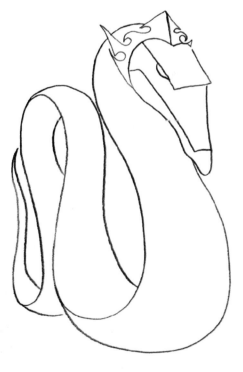

Use small triangles and wave shapes to create the outline of the crown.

Draw in simple outlines to start off the face. Sketch a rough rectangle for the bony head.

Instructions

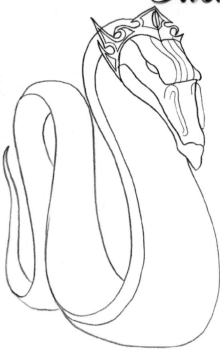

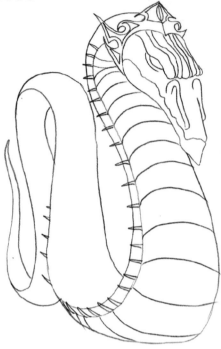

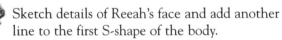

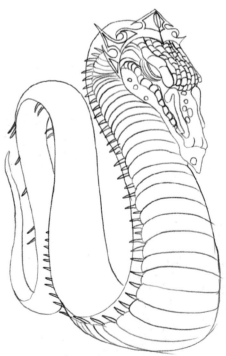

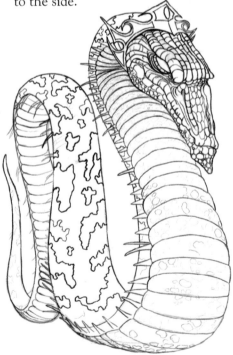

Sketch details of Reeah's face and add another line to the first S-shape of the body.

Add more details to the face and crown. Add rings to the front of the body and small spines to the side.

Add more rings and spines. Keep working on the face and head, paying close attention to the scales.

Add pattern and texture to your drawing. Finish off by giving Reeah a brown front and dark green coloring with splashes of brown over the rest of the body.

Variations

Color Drawing

STEP 1

1. On a large sheet of paper or board, use your ruler to draw in the straight lines for the castle towers and triangular shapes for the turrets.
2. Add small squares for the windows and draw a rough outline for the rocks in the foreground.
3. Sketch in six of the Ak-Baba in various positions around the castle to give depth—the seventh will be added in Step 8.

STEP 2

1. Add the blue sky. This will be the lightest part of your painting. The sky should be darker at the top of the page.
2. Paint in the green shapes for the hills in the background.
3. You can mix white with the green to highlight the tops of the hills.

STEP 3

1. Add darker greens and browns to the hills to give them more depth—but don't make them too dark.
2. The hills on the right of your painting should be lighter because they are further away.
3. Using small brush strokes, add in the darker detail of the trees to create a bit of texture to contrast with the smooth sky.

STEP 4

1. Look at different kinds of rocks and decide what your rocks in the foreground will look like.
2. Start with a relaxed, free hand and splash the paint on to build up texture. Like most random structures, rocks have a pattern that repeats itself.
3. Use a flat red to color in the turret roofs. Add a little white so the red is not too bright.

Color Drawing

STEP 5

1. Think about where the main light source is and remember that the surface closest to the light is a lighter color. Build up the cylindrical shape of the castle towers by shading with light gray.
2. Add darker gray on the side away from the light to emphasize the roundness of the towers.
3. Start to draw in the detail at the top of the towers and around the windows.

STEP 6

1. Finish off the castle by building up the shadows, but remember to be careful with the dark gray. Use less of it than the light gray.
2. Add texture to the castle walls.
3. Draw in more details of the ornamentation around the windows and turrets by adding more shadows to the patterns.

STEP 7

1. Color in your Ak-Baba, starting on the largest one in the foreground. This will be the brightest Ak-Baba, so you can use a bright orange for its body.
2. This Ak-Baba's mouth will also need to be bright, so start with your brightest red and use lighter and darker reds for the detail in the mouth.
3. Remember, to get bright colors, don't add any white or dilute them with water.

STEP 8

1. Block in the other five Ak-Baba using base colors of your choice and add detail of patterns and shadows. Remember that anything farther away gets lighter in color, so these Ak-Babas should be lighter than those in front.
2. Now you can see where to place the seventh Ak-Baba to add balance. The wings are the darkest part, so draw them in first.

Color Drawing

STEP 9

1. Color the beak and jaws of the Ak-Baba in the foreground and work on the smaller Ak-Baba in the background.
2. Now that your painting is nearly finished, you will notice that some areas work better than others. Think of the composition. The background should be the lightest part, so you can add clouds to make the sky lighter.
3. The Ak-Baba in the foreground is the focal point. You can add more details and bright colors to make it stand out.
4. Ak-Baba are very ferocious, so think of patterns and colors that look dangerous. Torn wing membranes make them look more vicious.

STEP 10

1. Adjust the colors to make things in the foreground stand out. Here the orange Ak-Baba stands out against its opposite color, blue, in the sky. You can also make things in the background blurry so they seem further away: Adding a fine mist of white achieves this effect.
2. Now you can use a little black—but very sparingly—to add depth to the shadows, particularly on those parts that are closest to us.
3. And remember: You will know when your painting is finished, so don't overwork it!

Dedicated to Andrew Berkhut,
who made this book possible.

MM

ISBN 0-439-73647-1

First published in 2004
Introduction and caption text copyright © Emily Rodda
Drawing instructions copyright © 2004 Marc McBride
Deltora Quest concept and characters copyright © Emily Rodda
Illustrations copyright © 2004 Marc McBride
Cover copyright © 2004 Scholastic Australia
Designed by Helen McKeon

All rights reserved. Published by Scholastic Inc., 557 Broadway, New York, NY 10012,
by arrangement with Scholastic Press, an imprint of Scholastic Australia.

SCHOLASTIC and associated logos are trademarks and/or registered trademarks of
Scholastic Inc.

12 11 10 9 8 7 6 5 4 3   5 6 7 8 9 10/0

Printed in the U.S.A.

First American edition, May 2005